PICNIC

Emily Arnold McCully

A Harper Trophy Book

HARPER & ROW, PUBLISHERS

Library of Congress Cataloging in Publication Data
McCully, Emily Arnold.
  Picnic.

  Summary: A little mouse gets lost on the way to a
family picnic.
  [1. Mice—Fiction.   2. Picnicking—Fiction
3. Stories without words]   I. Title.
PZ7.M478415Pi 1984   [E]   83-47913
ISBN 0-06-024099-7
ISBN 0-06-024100-4 (lib. bdg.)
ISBN 0-06-443199-1 (pbk.)

First Harper Trophy edition, 1989.

For Nat and Tad